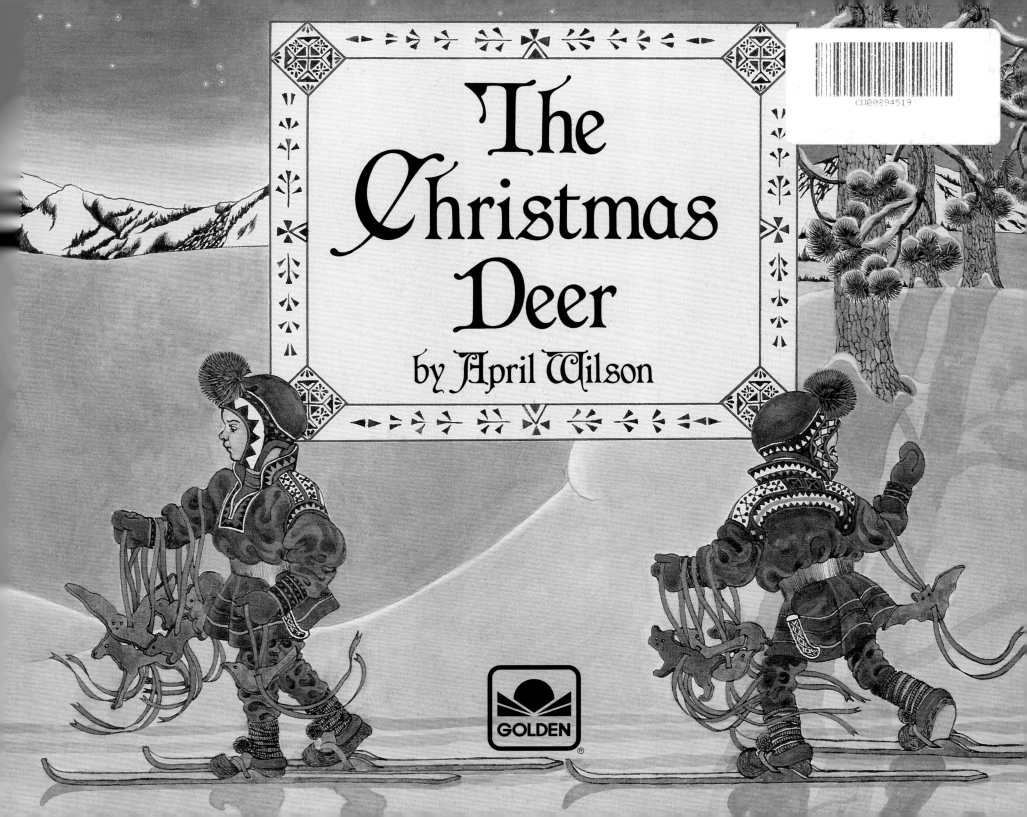

The Christmas Deer

by April Wilson

GOLDEN®

Winter had come to the far North. In the middle of a frozen forest a reindeer stood sleeping. He did not know that all around him a special magic was at work.

When the reindeer woke, he was surprised to find his antlers hung with strange shapes, strung on bright emerald ribbons. The first shape looked curiously like himself.

"What are these things?" he asked a flock of inquisitive birds.

"We don't know!" chirped one. "But they are very nice to eat. There is one shaped like a fox, and another like an owl. There's a hare and a raven and a wolf and a..."

But Reindeer wasn't listening. He was trying to clear his antlers of the shapes and the ribbons, but he could not shake them free.

Just then Fox came trotting up. "Hello!" he said. "Whatever are you doing Reindeer?"

"I am trying to rid myself of these things," the reindeer replied. "Do you know what they are?" Fox took a closer look but he had never seen anything like them before.

"They smell very tasty though," added Fox. "Do you mind if I eat one?"

"By all means," said Reindeer, and Fox gobbled the shape that looked like himself.

Owl flew by on silent wings and the animals stopped her.

"Owl, what are these strange things growing on Reindeer's antlers?" Fox asked, but he caught the scent of a hare before he could hear her answer, and dashed off to chase it. Owl peered at the shapes very closely. She wasn't too sure what they were, but she had a good idea who had put them there.

"They are not growing from your antlers," she said. "They have been put there for a special reason. You are honoured that they have been given to you."

"But what shall I do with them?" cried Reindeer, who wanted nothing more than his antlers to himself once more.

"They will lead you on a strange journey," said Owl. "There is one for every animal and bird in this forest — all you have to do is find them and give them away."

Fox returned with a struggling hare in his mouth. He was excited to hear about the mysterious journey. "I'll come with you, just as soon as I've eaten breakfast," said Fox, his eye on the terrified hare at his feet.

"There's no time for that," said Reindeer crossly. "Besides, Hare has a shape to eat on my antlers." So Fox let Hare go and she leapt to the safety of Reindeer's back as the little group set off through the snow.

They had not gone far when there was a movement in front of them. It was Lemming, burrowing along under the snow looking for mosses to eat. Suddenly, the sky crashed down upon him and he felt himself gripped by strong teeth.

Fox had pounced, but Fox wasn't having much luck with breakfast today. Reindeer had made a new rule — he would protect any animal who could find a shape to match them on his antlers, and luckily there was a shape for Lemming.

"That is a wise rule," said Owl, and even Fox reluctantly agreed. So Lemming joined Hare on Reindeer's back where he burrowed deep into the thick fur to enjoy eating his shape.

The group pressed on until they came to open ground. They were looking for shy Ptarmigan. With her winter-white feathers, she would be hard to find amongst the snow.

Up ahead, Ptarmigan had found an egg. She hadn't laid one lately, so it couldn't be hers. Besides, it wasn't the right time of year for eggs, when she had her white feathers on and there was so much snow. Still, just in case, she would bury it in a safe place. She was so busy digging that she didn't notice the little group come up behind her.

"Come with us, Ptarmigan," they cried. "You have a tasty shape to eat." Ptarmigan looked nervously at Fox for a moment, but Reindeer soon convinced her that she would be safe up on his back.

High above, Raven was watching. He wanted to know what Ptarmigan had buried. His mother had taught him that things carefully hidden are often good to eat. So he dived down and uncovered it.

He was so hungry that he swallowed his discovery whole. It stuck in his throat and was very uncomfortable. He flapped noisily about in the snow.

"Your greed has made you foolish," said Reindeer who had been watching. "You did not stop long enough to see that Ptarmigan's 'egg' was really a stone."

Raven was ashamed. But luckily he too had a shape on Reindeer's antlers and soon agreed to join the search.

Owl flew back with news of Brown Bear.

"He is inside the hollow tree after the bees' honey," said Owl. "He never learns." Sure enough, the animals could hear Bear's growls long before they saw him. Suddenly he roared passed, jaws dripping with honey, and a nose covered in stinging bees.

Reindeer was frightened of Bear, especially when he was angry.

"But Bear has a shape to be given," Owl reminded him. "You must be brave and go after him or you will never complete your task." So Reindeer swallowed his fear and soon found Bear rolling in the snow, desperately trying to cool his stinging nose.

Bear was pleased with his shape — it tasted almost as good as honey — so he too decided to join the strange procession.

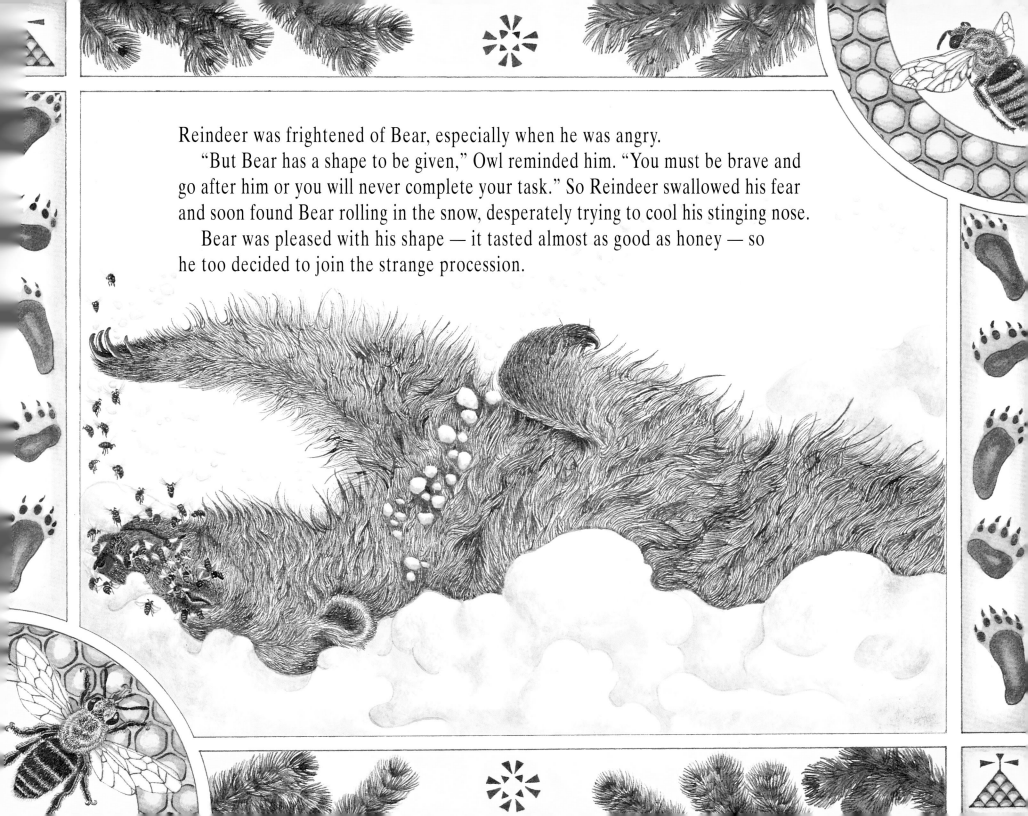

Bat was fed up. It had taken him ages to find a tree where he could spend the winter and now, because of Bear, it was full of angry bees. He was fluttering about, shrilling crossly, when Raven found him.

"Come with me," said Raven. "We have something for you." Soon Bat was happy again, hanging from his new resting place among Reindeer antler's.

"Who are we looking for next?" asked inquisitive Raven.

Reindeer had no time to answer, for suddenly Wolf was there, standing before them. Black Grouse was firmly between his jaws.

Reindeer was frightened when he saw Wolf for they were old enemies. But he remembered what Owl had told him and stepped forward.

"Why don't you join us?" he suggested. "But you must let Grouse go first."

"Why?" asked Wolf. "I am going to eat him."

"No you're not," said Bear. "You're going to let him go, and then you're going to come with us. You too, Grouse," he added. Wolf decided it was wise not to argue with Bear, so Grouse had a lucky escape that day.

Before the animals could decide who to look for next, "ping!" something hit Reindeer on the nose. The birds caught sight of Squirrel in the branches overhead. "Stop that!" they cried. "We are not after your pine cones. You're lucky we've found you, you have a..." But before they could finish, there was a cry from Reindeer.

"Look out!" he cried. "Behind you!" Squirrel had only just enough time to jump. He landed on Reindeer's back, where he chattered loudly at the branches above. Pine Marten glared angrily down at them. They had cheated him of a fine meal. But before long Reindeer had persuaded him to join them too.

In a forest clearing up ahead, the Badger Brothers were enjoying themselves. They had found a bush loaded with berries. They were barely halfway through eating them when Reindeer's group arrived. With cries of delight the birds swooped down upon the bush and soon had picked it clean.

"Never mind," said Reindeer to the disappointed badgers. "You have made the birds happy. Perhaps they will reward you." And he nodded to Bullfinch who flew down with a tasty shape for them to eat.

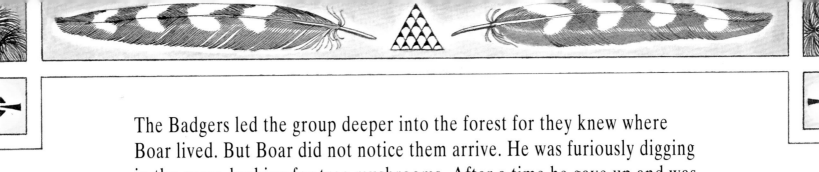

The Badgers led the group deeper into the forest for they knew where Boar lived. But Boar did not notice them arrive. He was furiously digging in the snow, looking for tree mushrooms. After a time he gave up and was surprised to see such an unlikely group of animals surrounding him.

"If you are after my mushrooms," he said gruffly, "you're too late."

"No, Boar. We have brought you something to eat instead," said Reindeer.

Free food was something never to be refused and Boar soon accepted.

Raven had flown on ahead. Now he returned with news of Lynx. He had found a set of her tracks.

"We must hurry if we are going to catch her," he advised. "She is moving fast up the mountainside." The animals groaned. The snow on the mountain was deep and dangerous.

"Owl, you and the others must wait for me here," said Reindeer firmly when they reached the mountain's lower slopes. "I will look for Lynx alone. After all, these are my gifts to give."

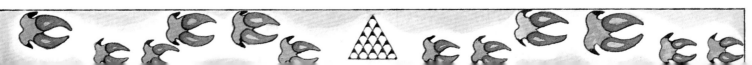

It took Reindeer a long while to find Lynx. It took him even longer to persuade her to come down from her hiding place among the trees.

"Please come with us," he pleaded.

"But Wolf and Bear are with you," said timid Lynx. "And they cannot be trusted."

"They can today," he assured her. "Today, all the animals of the forest must agree to be friends. And that means you too, Lynx!" he added, thinking of Squirrel and Hare. So Lynx agreed and together they headed back down the mountain.

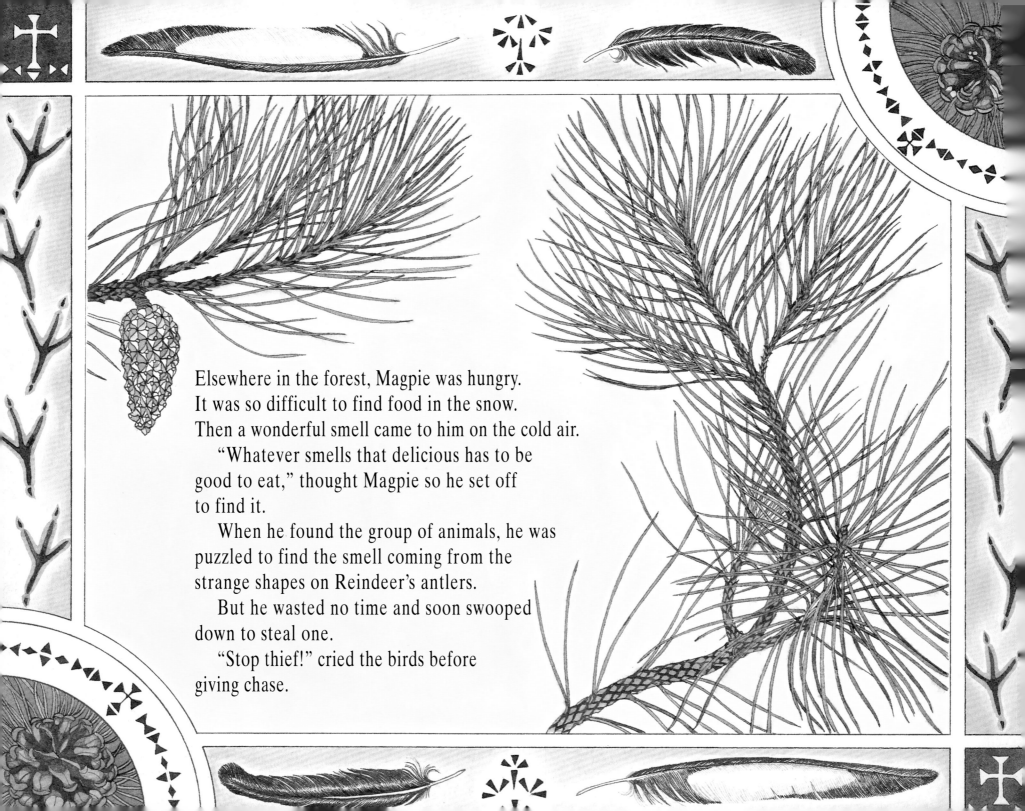

Elsewhere in the forest, Magpie was hungry.
It was so difficult to find food in the snow.
Then a wonderful smell came to him on the cold air.

"Whatever smells that delicious has to be
good to eat," thought Magpie so he set off
to find it.

When he found the group of animals, he was
puzzled to find the smell coming from the
strange shapes on Reindeer's antlers.

But he wasted no time and soon swooped
down to steal one.

"Stop thief!" cried the birds before
giving chase.

Owl was just about to follow when she spotted a little ermine beneath her, struggling in the deep snow. She flew on and, with alarm, saw that a large wolverine was creeping up silently behind the poor creature, choosing the exact moment to pounce.

Owl cried out in alarm but before she had time to turn back, Reindeer was there. He leapt down from a high bank of snow and stood his ground between snarling Wolverine and frightened Ermine.

"There is no need to fight," he said calmly. "We have food here for you both if you will agree to join us on a special journey." Ermine was only too happy to accept Reindeer's gift and, after some persuading by Owl, Wolverine agreed too.

The animals were just wondering what to do next when Raven and the other birds returned with a bewildered Magpie.

"Well, who must we look for now?" he asked, after Reindeer had explained the purpose of their strange quest.

"Elk," answered Owl and the animals fell silent for Elk was seldom seen in the forest itself. What's more, the great orange sun was dipping low towards the horizon, sending long black shadows across the snowy ground. It would soon be dark.

"We should head on along the forest edge," said Owl. "Follow me!"

They had not gone far when Lynx's sharp ears picked up a strange thrashing sound nearby. She and Reindeer struggled to the top of a ridge and were surprised to find two heads looking up at them from a deep snow drift.

"Elk calves!" laughed Reindeer. "They are the most careless of creatures." And the calves soon proved him right — for they had lost sight of their mother while playing and had jumped straight into the deep snow.

"You wait here with them, Lynx, while I fetch the others," instructed Reindeer. "Bear will dig them out."

Before long, the growing group of animals were walking along together.

Reindeer was almost beginning to enjoy himself. Now that they had found the elk calves, there were only two animals left to find. But one of them was Polar Bear! Most sensible animals will do their best to stay away from polar bears, and yet here they were trying to find one.

Their journey had taken the animals onto the shores of a frozen lake. As they stood there, silent in the gathering dusk, it began to snow. Ahead they heard cries. Out of the swirling flakes a furry white shape stumbled into them.

"Well, I think we have found our Polar Bear," said Reindeer.

The animals looked at the forlorn creature, and agreed that he wasn't nearly so huge and fierce as they had expected.

"There is a blizzard coming," Reindeer warned. "We must press on."

They were half way across the lake when they heard a deep growling. Looking behind him eagerly, Polar Bear stopped. Crashing into their midst came a huge white shape. It scattered the animals across the ice and, when they found each other again, Polar Bear was gone. They listened for his cries on the wind, but heard nothing.

"Poor lost Polar Bear," began Lynx.

"You needn't worry about him," laughed Reindeer. "He's just found his mother."

The animals decided that they weren't brave enough to go looking for polar bears twice in one day. "We can rest soon," said Reindeer. "There is another forest ahead."

Sure enough, just as the storm grew worse, the animals found themselves surrounded by trees again. "We can continue our search tomorrow," said Reindeer. "Tonight we can make snow dens and sleep."

Ermine was sniffing around, looking for a good place to dig his den, when he found some strange tracks. Without thinking, he followed them.

"What strange animal could have made these?" he wondered. He thought he knew all the tracks of the forest animals, but he had never seen any like these before.

Something moving under the snow caught his attention. He pounced and pulled out an angry Woodmouse clinging to a strange star shape, just like those on Reindeer's antlers.

"This is mine!" squealed Woodmouse bravely. "You find your own. There are lots of them up there." Ermine looked up and saw that the trees were filled with many different shapes strung onto coloured ribbons. They hung either side of the pathway made by the strange tracks. Leaving Woodmouse behind, Ermine raced back through the snow and fetched the others.

"I know what these tracks are," said Wolf sniffing at them. "They are made by humans."

"They must have very odd feet then," said Ermine, who had never seen a human before.

"They have 'snow feet'," Wolf replied. "They put them on when they wish to run fast."

"What strange creatures," Ermine said.

"And dangerous ones, too," added Wolf, who did not trust humans.

The animals stopped and looked uneasy, some muttering about turning back. "But we have come so far," said Reindeer. "If we turn back now we will never know what we were brought here for." They all agreed with this and Reindeer went in front just to show that he wasn't afraid.

Gradually, the trees thinned and they could see a glow ahead. There was a warmth too. Delicious smells teased their nostrils and almost without noticing they hurried their pace. Before they reached the clearing the deep voice of a man surprised them.

"Welcome, animals. Don't be afraid. I have been waiting for you."

He had a kind voice and spoke with words that they could understand. They didn't know why but they trusted his smiling face that was old and young at the same time.

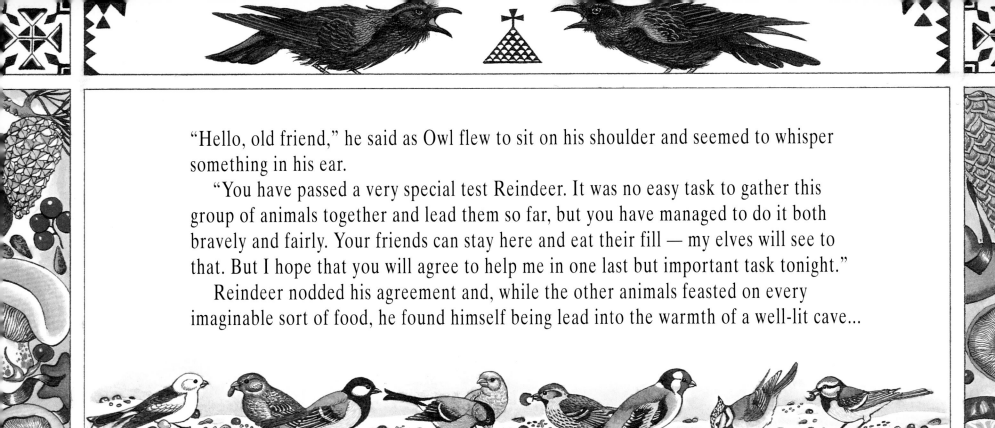

"Hello, old friend," he said as Owl flew to sit on his shoulder and seemed to whisper something in his ear.

"You have passed a very special test Reindeer. It was no easy task to gather this group of animals together and lead them so far, but you have managed to do it both bravely and fairly. Your friends can stay here and eat their fill — my elves will see to that. But I hope that you will agree to help me in one last but important task tonight."

Reindeer nodded his agreement and, while the other animals feasted on every imaginable sort of food, he found himself being lead into the warmth of a well-lit cave...

When Reindeer returned, the animals blinked in astonishment for he was decked in a beautiful harness and was pulling a splendid sleigh. The man raised his hand for silence.

"Animals, thank you all for coming to my feast tonight. If any of you wish to stay, we should be very glad of your company. You will always be safe here, for this is a very special forest. Now though, we must leave you, for we have many places to visit this night and far to travel."

With that, the man slipped into his "snow feet" and took up the reins that rang with countless silvery bells.

"Come my new-found friend, let us be off!" he cried as they leapt together into the darkness. "Merry Christmas to you all!"

"Goodbye!" called Reindeer, who was sad to be leaving his friends but excited by the adventure that lay ahead.

"Goodbye and safe return!" cried the animals in reply. And they listened until the tinkling bells no longer whispered on the north wind, and the sleigh disappeared at last into the dark, dark night.